To Baillea, Dottie and Margaret Z – *DS*

To Yumi and Chalky – *RR*

SIMON AND SCHUSTER
First published in Great Britain in 2012 by Simon and Schuster UK Ltd
1st Floor, 222 Gray's Inn Road, London WC1X 8HB
A CBS Company

Text copyright © 2012 Dyan Sheldon
Illustrations copyright © 2012 Rosie Reeve

Design by Jane Buckley

ISBN: 978-1-84738-707-3 (HB)
ISBN: 978-1-84738-708-0 (PB)

Printed in China
2 4 6 8 10 9 7 5 3 1

Something Magic
in the Night

Dyan Sheldon & Rosie Reeve

SIMON AND SCHUSTER
London New York Sydney Toronto New Delhi

The cookies are baked, the shopping done.
The tree is up, the balls are hung.

There are cards, and sweets, and baubles bright.
Everything's ready for Christmas night.

Nothing moves within the house.
Not parent nor cat; not child nor mouse.

The softest sounds, the faintest light,

Dark and quiet fill this night.

Something calls, and something sings.
Something whispers, something rings.
Something rustles, out of sight.

Something stirs within this night.

Dottie Sue sits up in bed.
She rubs her eyes and shakes her head.

Her heart beats fast, her head feels light.

There's **something** happening in this night.

It's Christmas Eve, there can't be more,
But still she crosses to the door.

The feeling's strong, she knows she's right.
There's **something** happening in this night.

Onto the landing and over the floor,
Past the room where her parents snore.

Down the stairs in the shadowy light.

What makes her so restless in this night?

It isn't the tree or the mistletoe.
It isn't the gifts tied in ribbons and bows.

It isn't the glittering tinsel so bright,
That sends her softly through this night.

And it isn't the wreaths or the silvery stars.
It isn't the garlands or long strings of cards.

It isn't the twinkling, coloured lights.

There's **something** different in this night.

Cries and whispers, laughter, song,
Bells are ringing loud and long.

Dottie Sue holds Bunny tight.

There's **something** different in this night.

Far away a baby cries,
Sweet angels sing and shepherds sigh.

And here the world is all alight.

For there's **something** magic in this night.

Beneath the sharply shining stars,
Creatures have come from near and far.

There they dance in the moonshine bright.
For there's **something** magic in this night.

She lets the stars and moon spill in,
And pulls the covers to her chin.

Her dreams overflow with pure delight,
Filled with the magic of this night.